MICHAEL TOWNSEND'S
AMAZING GREEK MYTHS
OF WONDER
AND BLUNDERS

WELCOME TO THE WONDERFUL
WORLD OF GREEK MYTHOLOGY

PUFFIN
An Imprint of Pengu...

PUFFIN BOOKS
An imprint of Penguin Young Readers Group
Published by the Penguin Group
Penguin Group (USA)
375 Hudson Street
New York, New York 10014, U.S.A.

USA / Canada / UK / Ireland / Australia / New Zealand / India / South Africa / China
Penguin Books Ltd, Registered Offices: 80 Strand, London WC2R 0RL, England

For more information about the Penguin Group visit www.penguin.com

First published in the United States of America by Dial Books for Young Readers,
a division of Penguin Young Readers Group, 2010
Published by Puffin Books, an imprint of Penguin Young Readers Group, 2014

Library of Congress Cataloging-in-Publication Data is available.
LC: 2010278984

Puffin Books ISBN 978-0-14-751069-3

Manufactured in China

1 3 5 7 9 10 8 6 4 2

The publisher does not have any control over and does not assume
any responsibility for author or third-party websites or their content.

ALWAYS LEARNING   PEARSON

TABLE OF CONTENTS

An Introduction . . . . page 5

The Foolish King Midas and the Golden Touch
page 18

Pandora and the Box of Mystery
page 40

Pygmalion and His Rocky Relationship!!!
page 52

The Abduction of Persephone
page 65

Arachne Gets a Big Head!!!
page 85

Perseus vs. Two Nasty Kings and a Really Ugly Monster
page 99

Pyramus and Thisbe: An Icky Love Story
page 113

The Short Flight of Icarus!
page 127

Hercules and the Ten Labors (Give or Take a Few)
page 140

The Drawn-Out Finale . . .
page 157

THE BOOK YOU ARE ABOUT TO READ CONTAINS NINE BIZARRE AND WACKY TALES THAT TAKE PLACE IN A GREEK-TASTIC MYTH-O-RIFIC WORLD!!! A WORLD THAT YOU, THE READER, MIGHT NOT BE FAMILIAR WITH. SO, LET'S BEGIN WITH A QUICK INTRODUCTION!!!...

6

7

8

THESE THINGS JUST DIDN'T EXIST YET...

IN FACT, NO ELECTRONICS OR MODERN MACHINES EXISTED YET.

10

BECAUSE THIS IS A QUICK INTRO, WE WON'T BE ABLE TO MEET ALL THE GODS (THERE ARE WAY TOO MANY). WE'LL JUST MEET A SELECT FEW, STARTING WITH ZEUS AND HERA.

ZEUS WAS BY FAR THE MOST POWERFUL OF ALL THE GODS. HE RULED MIGHTILY OVER THE HEAVENS WITH THE HELP OF HIS TRUSTY LIGHTNING BOLTS.

I THINK I TAUGHT THAT MORTAL A LESSON... BUT JUST IN CASE, HAND ME ANOTHER LIGHTNING BOLT!!!

HERA WAS ZEUS'S FAVORITE WIFE (BUT NOT HIS ONLY WIFE). SHE WAS A VERY JEALOUS WOMAN WHO DID NOT WANT TO SHARE ZEUS'S LOVE WITH ANYONE ELSE.

ZEUS SAID I LOOKED PRETTY TODAY.

HE SAID THE SAME TO ME!!!

GRRRR

KA-POOF

HERA'S JEALOUSY OFTEN LED HER TO DO VERY MEAN THINGS.

HEE HEE HEE

? ?

14

16

MMMM

I SURE DO LOVE YOU, YUMMY CHICKEN... ALMOST AS MUCH AS I LOVE...

EXCUSE ME, KING MIDAS!

YES

I'M SORRY TO INTERRUPT YOUR MID-DAY SNACK...

BUT I THINK YOU SHOULD COME AND SEE WHAT WE JUST FOUND IN YOUR ROYAL ROSE GARDENS...

WAS IT GOLD?

UM...NO

THEN I REALLY DON'T CARE!!!

I GOT LOST **HICCUP**

WELL, I'LL HELP YOU FIND THEM!

BUT I CAN'T RETURN YOU TO DIONYSUS ALL SAD AND STUFF...

HMMM

I KNOW! WE'LL EAT CHICKEN TILL YOU CHEER UP!

SNIFF?

SO MIDAS HAD A HUGE BANQUET SET UP...

AND THEY BEGAN TO EAT...

MUNCH MUNCH MUNCH

MUNCH MUNCH MUNCH

AND EAT...

-BURP-

MUNCH MUNCH MUNCH

MUNCH MUNCH MUNCH

MMMM... CHICKEN

AND EAT

MUNCH MUNCH MUNCH

-BURP-

AND EAT

-BURP-

-BURP-

MUNCH MUNCH MUNCH

MUNCH MUNCH MUNCH

25

26

27

WHEN THE CELEBRATION FINALLY ENDED, DIONYSUS APPROACHED KING MIDAS.

SO, HAVE YOU DECIDED WHAT YOU WANT?

YUP!

I WANT TO TURN THINGS TO GOLD WITH MY TOUCH!

HA HA HA

YOU'RE KIDDING, RIGHT?

UM... NO.

VERY WELL, I'LL GRANT YOUR WISH... BUT I'M WARNING YOU...

HEE HEE HEE

YAY

MIDAS WAS SO EXCITED HE RAN ALL THE WAY HOME TO TEST OUT HIS NEW GIFT!!!

MIDAS, YOUR HORSE

BYE, SILENUS!

A SHORT TIME LATER, IN THE KING'S PALACE...

PANT PANT
HEE HEE
PANT PANT

HERE IT GOES!

HEE HEE HEE

FWINGLE

IT WORKS

HEE HEE HA HA HA

I AM GOING TO HAVE SOOO MUCH FUN!

AND KING MIDAS DID HAVE FUN. LOTS AND LOTS OF FUN.

HEE HEE

FWINGLE

HA HA HA

FWINGLE

SHINY!

FWINGLE

THIS IS THE BEST DAY OF MY LIFE!

MEOW

FWINGLE

HEE HEE

FWINGLE

FWINGLE

HEE HEE

FWINGLE

FWINGLE

HA

SIGH

HA

HA

KITTY?

THE KING WORKED TIRELESSLY TURNING EVERYTHING TO GOLD UNTIL HE GOT A LOUD AND URGENT MESSAGE FROM HIS TUMMY.

GRUMBLE

HUH?

WHAT IS IT, TUMMY? ARE YOU HUNGRY?

GRUMBLE

SERVANTS!!! MY TUMMY IS HUNGRY! PREPARE US A FEAST WITH LOTS OF TASTY CHICKEN,

AND SO THE KING'S MEN PREPARED A GIANT FEAST. THE KING EAGERLY PICKED UP HIS SILVER... ERR... GOLDENWARE, READY TO DIG IN.

MMMM...

HUH?

TWINGLE

31

BUT WHEN HE WENT TO TAKE HIS FIRST BITE...

HE REALIZED HE HAD A PROBLEM...

FWINGLE CRUNCH

A BIG PROBLEM.

OWWW!

THINGS ONLY GOT WORSE WHEN HE WENT TO SIP HIS ROYAL WINE.

FWINGLE COUGH COUGH

KING MIDAS WAS STARTING TO WORRY...

THIS IS NOT GOOD. NOT GOOD AT ALL. WHAT AM I GOING TO DO?

CRASH

HUNGRY, TIRED, AND THIRSTY, HE WENT TO LIE DOWN AND REST.

GROAN!

GRUMBLE

FWINGLE

BUT KING MIDAS QUICKLY REALIZED IT'S HARD TO REST ON A GOLDEN BED.

GROAN

THINGS COULDN'T BE ANY WORSE!

GRUMBLE

A SHORT TIME LATER, BACK AT DIONYSUS'S CAMP...

HA HA HA HA HA HA
THAT IS TOTALLY HOW A MONKEY WOULD DANCE!

OHHH OHHH AH AH AH OHHH

GURGLE

HUH?

WHAT WAS THAT?

IT'S ME, KING MIDAS.

WHAT ARE YOU DOING BACK HERE?

35

WELL, IT LOOKS LIKE YOU MADE A TRUE FRIEND OUT OF SILENUS BECAUSE...

HE'S SUGGESTED THAT I REVOKE YOUR WISH IN EXCHANGE FOR A VERY SPECIAL DANCE NUMBER PUT ON BY THE BOTH OF YOU.

GURGLE

UM... OKAY.

AND SO, AFTER A BIT OF REHERSAL, MIDAS AND SILENUS WERE READY TO PERFORM A VERY SPECTACULAR DUCKY DANCE!

HE HE HE

THAT IS SOOO HOW DUCKS WOULD DANCE.

QUACK QUACK QUACK

QUACK QUACK QUACK

37

DIONYSUS LOVED THE PERFORMANCE, ESPECIALLY THE BIG SPLASH ENDING IN THE FORMERLY MUDDY PACTOLUS RIVER.

SPLASH

FWINGLE

AND HE HAPPILY CURED MIDAS OF HIS "GOLDEN TOUCH" AND EVEN SENT HIM ON HIS WAY WITH A BUNCH OF GIFT CHICKENS!!!

WOW, CHECK OUT THE SPARKLY SANDS!

GOODBYE

BYE!

BYE

THE FIRST THING KING MIDAS DID WHEN HE GOT HOME WAS GIVE HIS LITTLE PRINCESS A BIG, BIG HUG.

THEN HE ATE SOME OF HIS GIFT CHICKENS.

HEY DADDY, PLEASE PROMISE ME YOU'LL NEVER MAKE A FOOLISH WISH EVER AGAIN!

MUNCH MUNCH MUNCH

I PROMISE!

41

YOU'RE SOOO RIGHT, KITTY.

WHO AM I KIDDING? THIS IS GOING TO BE TORTURE!

ALL DAY LONG PANDORA DESPERATELY TRIED TO KEEP HERSELF BUSY.

BUT NO MATTER WHAT SHE DID...

LICK LICK LICK

BOOK

SHE COULDN'T KEEP HER MIND OFF THE BOX!!!

MEOW

42

SHE EVEN TRIED GOING FOR A LONG WALK...

BUT THAT DIDN'T HELP EITHER, BECAUSE EVERYWHERE SHE LOOKED...

SHE WOULD STILL SEE THE BOX.

OPEN ME, PANDORA?

NOOOOO!

43

EXTREMELY FRUSTRATED, PANDORA TRIED TO ESCAPE BY GOING TO BED. BUT SHE COULDN'T SLEEP, SHE COULD ONLY IMAGINE WHAT WONDERFUL MYSTERIES THE BOX MIGHT HOLD.

FINALLY, IN THE MIDDLE OF PANDORA'S SLEEPLESS NIGHT... SHE SNAPPED.

WHO IN THE WORLD GIVES A GIFT YOU CAN'T OPEN?

I WONDER HOW ZEUS WOULD LIKE IT...

IF I GAVE HIM A BOX...

AND TOLD HIM HE COULDN'T OPEN IT!

AND SO PANDORA SET ABOUT MAKING HER OWN BOX TO GIVE TO ZEUS.

HA HA HA HA HA HA HA HA HA

BANG BANG

45

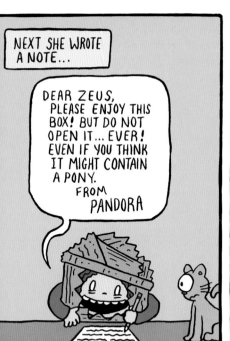

NEXT SHE WROTE A NOTE...

DEAR ZEUS,
PLEASE ENJOY THIS BOX! BUT DO NOT OPEN IT... EVER! EVEN IF YOU THINK IT MIGHT CONTAIN A PONY.
FROM
PANDORA

BEFORE PANDORA LEFT HER HOME, SHE WALKED PAST HER BOX ONE LAST TIME.

WOW
IT'S LIKE I'M LOOKING IN A MIRROR!

AS SHE STARED AT THE BOX SHE GOT YET ANOTHER IDEA!

WHY DIDN'T I THINK OF THIS BEFORE?

I'LL OPEN THE BOX IN MY DISGUISE!

THAT WAY I'LL NEVER GET CAUGHT!

HA HA HA
HA HA HA
HA HA
HA HA HA

PANDORA SCRAMBLED OUT OF HER DISGUISE AND RUSHED TO SHUT THE BOX.

UGGG!

SLAM

PANT PANT PANT

YOU OKAY, KITTY?

49

YOU SEE, SHE HAD REPLACED THE LID JUST IN TIME TO KEEP HOPE FROM ESCAPING.

HOPE

AND SO THANKS TO PANDORA WE NOW HAVE EVIL APLENTY IN OUR WORLD, BUT AT LEAST WE STILL HAVE HOPE.

I SURE **HOPE** WE FIND PANDORA SOON!

YEAH, ME TOO.

AND I **HOPE** THEY EVENTUALLY GIVE UP!

THE HOPEFUL END

IN THE LAND OF CYPRUS THERE WAS A FAMOUS SCULPTOR NAMED PYGMALION.

CHIP CHIP CHIP CHIP

HIS SCULPTURES WERE FAMOUS FOR BEING SO LIFELIKE THAT IF YOU CAME ACROSS THEM OUTSIDE OF HIS STUDIO...

CHIP CHIP CHIP CHIP CHIP

YOU WOULD NEVER GUESS THEY WERE STONE!

HEY, I THINK MY HORSE IS BROKEN.

QUACK QUACK*

*TRANSLATION: LIFEGUARD, HELP! A DROWNING DUCK!

EEEK

MONSTER!

DAY IN AND DAY OUT, PYGMALION REMAINED IN HIS STUDIO HAPPILY CHIPPING AWAY.

HEY PYGGY! YOU WANNA JOIN US ON AN ADVENTURE?

NO THANKS!

ARE YOU SURE?

WE'RE GOING TO THROW ROCKS AT BIG ANIMALS!

IT'LL BE FUN

NO THANKS.

AND ALTHOUGH PYGMALION WORKED ALONE, HE DIDN'T FEEL ALONE AROUND ALL HIS STATUES.

OKAY GUYS, STOP ME IF YOU'VE HEARD THIS ONE...

HOW MANY CENTAURS DOES IT TAKE TO SCREW IN A LIGHTBULB?

YOU GIVE UP...?

THE ANSWER IS NONE...

BECAUSE LIGHTBULBS DON'T EXIST!

HA HA HA HA HA!

OKAY, TIME TO GET BACK TO WORK.

IF YOU THINK IT'S WEIRD THE WAY PYGMALION TALKED TO HIS STATUES, YOU WOULD BE RIGHT. BECAUSE IT WAS.

HMMM... WHAT'S NEXT?

ORDER FORM
☑ 6 LIONS
☑ 4 SOLDIERS
☐ A PRETTY GIRL IN A DRESS

AND THE LONGER PYGMALION REMAINED ALONE, THE WEIRDER THINGS GOT.

HOLD STILL— ALMOST DONE.

CHIP CHIP CHIP

UNTIL ONE AFTERNOON, THE STRANGEST THING HAPPENED.

WOW YOU'RE PRETTY

HE FELL MADLY IN LOVE WITH ONE OF HIS STATUES.

HI, I'M PYGMALION, DO YOU WANNA GO OUT SOMETIME?

FOR THE NEXT SEVERAL DAYS PYGMALION TRIED TO WIN OVER HIS NEW LOVE !!!

IF YOU AGREE, I'LL GIVE YOU A DRESS!

HEY BEAUTIFUL! DO YOU LIKE PONIES?

NEIGH

HE GAVE HER PRESENTS.

HE WROTE HER LOVE SONGS.

LA LA LA LA LA LA I LOVE YOU TEN TIMES MORE THAN A MONKEY LOVES BANANAS. LA LA LA LA LA LA

HE EVEN TRIED A LITTLE HIP-HOP.

YO-GIRL YOU HARD AS ICE BUT I THINK YOU BE NICE WORD.

HIP

HOP

BUT NO MATTER WHAT HE TRIED, THE STATUE DIDN'T ANSWER.

PLEASE ANSWER ME MY LOVE!

SOB SOB SOB SOB SOB SOB

MUNCH MUNCH MUNCH MUNCH MUNCH

58

OVERCOME WITH SADNESS, PYGMALION STOPPED WORKING.

SNIFF SNIFF

THE NORMAL NOISES OF HIS WORK STOPPED...

CHIP CHIP CHIP CHIP CHIP CHIP CHIP

AND WERE REPLACED BY A NEW NOISE.

SOB SOB SOB SOB SOB SOB SOB SOB

MEANWHILE...

HEY! WHERE IS MY PRETTY GIRL STATUE?

UMM... IT HASN'T ARRIVED YET.

WELL, I HAVE DEADLINES TO MEET, SO UNLESS YOU WANT TO PUT ON A DRESS AND FILL THE VOID...

GET ME MY STATUE!

YES, SIR.

THE WORKER RACED OFF TO PYGMALION'S STUDIO, BUT NOBODY WAS HOME... AT LEAST, NOT PYGMALION.

KNOCK KNOCK

ANYONE HOME?

NEIGH

SO HE FRANTICALLY SEARCHED HIGH AND LOW FOR PYGMALION UNTIL HE FINALLY FOUND HIM COMING OUT OF APHRODITE'S TEMPLE.

THERE YOU ARE!

PIGGY! WHAT ARE YOU DOING OUTSIDE OF YOUR STUDIO?

I WAS MAKING A REQUEST TO APHRODITE, THE GODDESS OF LOVE.

WHAT KIND OF REQUEST?

60

61

APHRODITE DID IT! SHE HEARD YOUR REQUEST AND THOUGHT IT WAS CUTE... AND **SO DO I !!!**

HOORAY!

THIS IS CREEPY... I'M LEAVING.

OH, AND I'M GOING TO BORROW THIS DRESS.

WITHIN HOURS PYGMALION AND HIS LOVE GOT MARRIED.

WOW! WHAT A ROCK!

THANKS, I CARVED IT MYSELF!

TODAY WAS THE LAST DAY OF HADES' VACATION IN "THE LAND OF THE LIVING"

THEN HE HAD TO RETURN TO HIS KINGDOM...

SIGH

THE DREARY "LAND OF THE DEAD," ALSO KNOWN AS THE "UNDERWORLD."

SIR, WHY DO YOU LOOK SO SAD?

WELL, DEADKINS, I'M JUST REALIZING HOW MUCH I'M GOING TO MISS BEING AROUND ALL THESE LIVING THINGS!

HI BUNNY.

GEE, IF ONLY WE COULD HAVE THE BEST OF BOTH WORLDS...

WAIT A SECOND!

WHY CAN'T WE?!?

LET'S BRING VACATION HOME!

DEADKINS, WRITE THIS DOWN.

I WANT FLOWERS, FRUIT TREES, AND MORE BUNNIES, LOTS MORE BUNNIES.

NOW, START COLLECTING!!!

YES, SIR.

AS DEADKINS ROUNDED UP ALL KINDS OF LIVELY STUFF, HADES ACTUALLY BEGAN TO LOOK FORWARD TO RETURNING HOME.

BUT, UNFORTUNATELY, THINGS WOULD NOT WORK OUT LIKE HE HOPED.

A FEW DAYS LATER...

SIGH

CHEER UP, SIR.

IF YOU WANT I CAN GO GET YOU SOME NEW FLOWERS.

NO NEED. THEY'LL JUST DIE TOO.

WELL, CAN I GET SOME MORE BUNNIES?

NO, CERBERUS WILL JUST EAT THEM TOO.

← CERBERUS IS HADES' 3-HEADED DOG

HOW ABOUT I GET SOME NEW FRUIT TREES?

THERE'S NO POINT, DEADKINS. NOTHING WILL LIVE DOWN HERE.

WELL, SIR, YOU'LL ALWAYS HAVE OUR UNDERWORLD FRUIT TREES!!!

OH, THEY'RE NOT THE SAME. THEY LOOK HORRIBLE AND ONLY THE DEAD CAN EAT THE FRUIT.

AND EVEN THEY DON'T LIKE IT.

YUCK

ACKK

I WISH I KNEW HOW MY SISTER KEEPS EVERYTHING LIVING UP THERE!

HEY, WE SHOULD SPY ON HER TO FIND OUT HER SECRET!

UM

A QUICK REMINDER: DEMETER (HADES' SISTER) IS THE GODDESS OF THE HARVEST.

BUT FIRST, WE NEED DISGUISES.

69

IT WAS BECAUSE EVERYONE'S EYES WERE ON DEMETER'S DAUGHTER, PERSEPHONE...

ARE YOU READY?

HMMMM

WHO WAS ABOUT TO PERFORM HER SPECIAL "HAPPY SONG AND DANCE."

YES   YES   YES   OKAY

IT BEGAN WITH A BIG SOLO...

HAPPY LA LA LA

FOLLOWED BY SOME FANCY FOOTWORK. WITH EVERY STEP, NEW LIFE SEEMED TO JUST POP UP!

LA LA LA

POP POP POP

POP POP POP

HADES WAS COMPLETELY CAPTIVATED BY PERSEPHONE.

LA LA LA

POP POP POP POP

CLAP CLAP CLAP CLAP CLAP CLAP CLAP CLAP

TA-DA

PANT PANT PANT

WOW!

OKAY, HUMAN WORKERS, TIME TO GET BACK TO WORK!!!

BOOO

HISS

HEY MOM?

CAN I HAVE A SNACK?

OF COURSE, MY LOVE!

CRUNCH

CHEW CHEW CHEW CHEW

WITH DEMETER DISTRACTED, HADES WAS FREE TO QUICKLY SWOOP IN, GRAB PERSEPHONE...

HA HA HA

RUMBLE

AND DISAPPEAR TO THE UNDERWORLD QUICKER THAN...

A RABBIT DOWN A RABBIT HOLE.

OFF IN THE DISTANCE, DEMETER INSTANTLY REALIZED SOMETHING WAS WRONG.

EVERYONE SHUT UP!

WHERE'S MY BABY?

75

DEMETER IMMEDIATELY BEGAN TO SEARCH THE WORLD OVER FOR HER DAUGHTER.

PERSEPHONE!

AND WITH ALL HER FOCUS ON HER SEARCH, SHE NEGLECTED THE NEEDS OF THE LAND AND A LIFELESS COLD TOOK OVER.

LEAVING NO WORK FOR THE WORKERS.

SO THIS IS A VACATION.

THIS IS SO **NOT** AWESOME.

THAT GIANT BUNNY IS A LIAR.

CHATTER CHATTER

CHATTER CHATTER

CHATTER CHATTER

77

OF COURSE, THINGS WEREN'T GOING TO GET BETTER, AND HIGH UP ON MOUNT OLYMPUS ZEUS SAW THAT CLEARLY.

HEY HERMES!

YES, MR. ZEUS, SIR?

I'M SICK AND TIRED OF MY KINGDOM BEING ALL ICY AND COLD...

GO TELL HADES TO RETURN PERSEPHONE TO HER MOTHER RIGHT AWAY... OR ELSE!

YES, SIR!

AND SO HERMES FLEW DOWN TO THE UNDERWORLD...

TO GIVE HADES ZEUS'S MESSAGE.

BLAH BLAH BLAH BLAH BLAH OR ELSE!

78

AFTER HERMES DELIVERED THE MESSAGE, HADES WAS HEARTBROKEN... BUT PERSEPHONE WAS VERY, VERY HAPPY!

NOOOOO

YAAAAY

SO HAPPY, SHE FELT THE NEED TO DO HER SONG AND DANCE

HAPPY LA-LA LA

LA LA LA

P POP POP

LA LA LA LA

POP POP POP TWIRL POP POP

I NEED TO DO SOMETHING... AND QUICK!

80

WHEN ZEUS FOUND OUT WHAT HAPPENED, HE WAS VERY ANNOYED.

WHY DIDN'T YOU STOP HER?

IT HAPPENED SO QUICK!

WELL, THE RULES ARE CLEAR...

ONCE YOU EAT THE FOOD OF THE DEAD, YOU CAN'T LEAVE THE UNDERWORLD.

BUT WHAT ABOUT DEMETER? WITHOUT PERSEPHONE, THE WORLD WILL REMAIN A GIANT ICE CUBE.

HMMMM...

HERMES, GO GET EVERYONE INVOLVED AND I'LL SOLVE THIS MESS ONCE AND FOR ALL.

RIGHT AWAY!

A SHORT TIME LATER...

OKAY, EVERYONE! I DON'T HAVE MUCH TO SAY, EXCEPT...

BABY!

MOMMY!

HADES, YOU SHOULDN'T HAVE KIDNAPPED PERSEPHONE!

AND PERSEPHONE, YOU SHOULD LOOK BEFORE YOU EAT!

SO, HERE'S WHAT I'VE DECIDED IS GOING TO HAPPEN.

PERSEPHONE, SINCE YOU ATE THE FOOD OF THE DEAD YOU **MUST** REMAIN WITH HADES AS HIS QUEEN. **BUT,** ONCE A YEAR, I WILL ALLOW YOU A REALLY, REALLY LONG VACATION WITH YOUR MOMMY, AND THAT'S **FINAL!**

NOW LET'S HAVE A HAPPY GROUP HUG!

GRRRR

I SAID HAPPY!

GRRRR

YAY!

YAY!

MEET ARACHNE!

ARACHNE WAS A WEAVER, AND A VERY GOOD ONE AT THAT.

HELLO!

SHE WAS SOOO GOOD THAT PEOPLE FROM ALL OVER WOULD COME JUST TO WATCH HER WORK.

ALL DONE!

WOW

CLAP

IT'S AWESOME!

HOORAY

CLAP

OH COME ON EVERYONE... STOP IT...

SERIOUSLY, YOU'RE EMBARRASSING ME!

HEE HEE HEE

86

SOME OF HER ADMIRERS LOVED HER SO MUCH, THEY EVEN FORMED A FAN CLUB.

HEY ARACHNE! WE'RE YOUR NEW FAN CLUB, THE "ARACHNE ADDICTS."

AND WE THINK YOU SHOULD ENTER THIS YEAR'S LOCAL WEAVING CONTEST!

AND IF YOU WIN YOU'LL BE A LOCAL CELEBRITY!

OH, I DON'T NEED TO BE FAMOUS, GUYS.

I'M JUST HAPPY TO BE ABLE TO KEEP FOOD ON MY TABLE.

UNFORTUNATELY FOR ARACHNE HER FANS STUCK AROUND, HOPING SHE MIGHT CHANGE HER MIND.

DO IT
DO IT
DO IT

DO IT
DO IT
DO IT

DO IT
DO IT
DO IT

DO IT
DO IT
DO IT

AND IT WASN'T LONG TILL ARACHNE BEGAN TO BELIEVE ALL THE HYPE ABOUT HERSELF.

WOW! YOU'RE SO AWESOME.

AND PRETTY.

AND SO TALENTED!

HEY, TRY THESE ON!

AND IT SHOWED... OH, DID IT SHOW!!!

HEY EVERYONE, I GOT A QUESTION! WHO'S THE MASTER OF THE LOOM?

YOU ARE!

YOU ARE!

YOU ARE!

AND WHO DESERVES ALL YOUR MONEY AND PRAISE?

YOU DO!

YOU DO!

YOU DO!

THAT'S CORRECT, NOW DON'T YOU FORGET IT! ARACHNE OUT!

BECAUSE ARACHNE CONTINUED WINNING ALL THE CONTESTS SHE ENTERED, IT WASN'T LONG BEFORE SHE HAD BEAT EVERY MORTAL WEAVER THERE WAS...

THE WINNER!

YEAH, YEAH, GIVE ME.

BUT STRANGELY, SHE WASN'T HAPPY.

BACK AT ARACHNE'S NEW MANSION...

WOW, YOU DID IT, ARACHNE! YOU'RE THE BEST MORTAL WEAVER EVER!!!

YEAH... BUT I WANT MORE!

SAY, WHO'S THE BEST WEAVER AMONG THE GODS?

UM... ATHENA, BY FAR.

WELL THAT'S IT, THEN!

I HEREBY CHALLENGE THE GODDESS ATHENA TO A WEAVE-OFF!

GASP!

AN EERIE SILENCE IMMEDIATELY FOLLOWED ARACHNE'S BOLD STATEMENT, UNTIL A STRANGER FROM THE BACK OF THE CROWD SPOKE UP.

EXCUSE ME, ARACHNE, BUT CHALLENGING A GOD IS A VERY UNWISE THING TO DO...

WHERE'D SHE COME FROM?

?

BUT I'M SURE IT'S NOT TOO LATE TO TAKE BACK WHAT YOU SAID AND BEG FOR MERCY.

OH, I MEANT WHAT I SAID, YOU STRANGE, GLOWING, MYSTERIOUS OLD LADY!

I WANT TO CHALLENGE ATHENA!

VERY WELL, THEN!

FLASH

94

THIS MEANT IT WAS JUDGMENT TIME! THEY BEGAN WITH ATHENA'S TAPESTRY FIRST.

IT SHOWED THE GODS IN ALL THEIR TRUE GLORY—AND IT REMINDED ARACHNE HOW LITTLE AND POWERLESS SHE ACTUALLY WAS!!!

OH, MY! WHAT WAS I THINKING?

OKAY, NOW LET'S GO SEE YOURS.

WAIT! THERE'S NO NEED, I FORFEIT. YOU WIN! JUST DON'T LOOK AT MY...

THERE! NOW YOU HAVE A TINY LITTLE HEAD.

PROBLEM SOLVED! HEE HEE HEE

!

WELL, I GOTTA GO NOW...

BUT I HOPE YOU LEARNED YOUR LESSON!

DO BUNNIES MAKE WARM HATS?

UM... I MEAN YES, I LEARNED MY LESSON.

SO EVEN THOUGH ARACHNE WAS NOW A SPIDER, SHE KNEW HOW LUCKY SHE WAS TO BE ALIVE.

AND AT LEAST I STILL GET TO WEAVE!

FROM THAT DAY FORTH SHE WAS VERY, VERY CAREFUL TO NOT DEVELOP ANY NEW BIG HEAD PROBLEMS!

HEY, LOOK AT THAT! IT'S BEAUTIFUL.

IT'S MESMERIZING. LET'S GET CLOSER!

I WANT TO TOUCH IT!!!

98

ONCE THERE WAS A NASTY KING NAMED ACRISIUS (OF ARGOS) WHO, ON A VISIT TO AN ORACLE, GOT SOME VERY BAD NEWS.

DANAË, YOUR DAUGHTER, WILL ONE DAY HAVE A BEAUTIFUL BABY BOY!!!

WHO WILL ONE DAY KILL YOU!

THANK YOU, COME AGAIN. (IF YOU'RE STILL ALIVE!)

BOY I HOPE SHE'S WRONG...

SADLY, FOR THE KING, ORACLES WERE NEVER WRONG!

BUT THAT DIDN'T STOP HIM FROM ATTEMPTING TO PREVENT HIS DAUGHTER FROM EVER HAVING A BABY!

GRRR   GRRRR   GRRRR   GRRR   GRRRR

GRRRR

RABID GUARD ANIMALS!

HA HA HA

STAY AWAY

A SAD PRINCESS IN HER NEW UNDER-GROUND PRISON.

SOB SOB SOB

100

THE KING HAD TRULY DONE A GREAT JOB AT KEEPING THE MORTALS AT BAY...

HUH?

POOF

BUT NOTHING HE COULD DO WOULD EVER KEEP THE MIGHTY ZEUS FROM HELPING A LONELY, PRETTY PRINCESS IN NEED!

HI THERE, PRINCESS, I'M HERE TO HELP YOU!

POOF

WOW, I'M PREGNANT!

NOW YOU WON'T BE LONELY!

THANKS ZEUS!

SOMETIME LATER, A BABY WAS BORN. DANAË NAMED HIM PERSEUS. SHE ALSO REALIZED HIDING A BABY ISN'T EASY.

HEY, I KNOW THAT SMELL!

GROSS

DANAË! DID YOU HAVE A BABY?

UM... MAYBE.

101

SINCE THE KING KNEW THAT THE FATE OF THOSE WHO KILL THEIR OWN FLESH AND BLOOD WAS WORSE THAN DEATH, HE DECIDED TO KILL THEM INDIRECTLY...

BY SENDING THEM ON A CRUISE.

BON VOYAGE!

SOB SOB SOB

WAAAA

NOT A REAL CRUISE SHIP.

HA HA HA HA HA

THEY'RE AS GOOD AS DEAD!

ONCE AGAIN THE KING'S PLAN FAILED. THE BOX WASHED ASHORE ON A SMALL ISLAND AND WAS FOUND BY AN OLD FISHING COUPLE.

GEE. I WONDER WHAT'S INSIDE?

MAYBE IT'S A PONY!

CRACK

EVEN BETTER! I ALWAYS WANTED CHILDREN!

WHOA, WHAT'S THAT SMELL?

FOR THE NEXT SEVERAL YEARS THE FOUR LIVED HAPPILY AS A FISHING FAMILY.

LOOK MA NO BOAT!

ARRR

UNTIL ONE DAY THE ISLAND'S EVIL KING POLYDECTES DECIDED TO MAKE PERSEUS'S PRETTY MOTHER HIS WIFE. BUT THERE WAS A SLIGHT PROBLEM.

ANOTHER FISH FAILS TO ESCAPE MY PATENTED "PIRATE FISH EYE GRAB"

THAT BOY SCARES ME!

CLAP CLAP CLAP

THE KING DIDN'T WANT A SCARY STEPSON.

SO HE DEVISED A COMPLEX PLAN TO GET RID OF PERSEUS.

HEY PERSEUS, I'LL GIVE YOU THIS CAKE IF YOU DO ME A FAVOR.

MMMM

OKAY, SO WHAT'S THE FAVOR?

LET'S SHAKE FIRST.

A BINDING HANDSHAKE

HEE HEE I WANT YOU TO GET ME THE HEAD OF MEDUSA THE GORGON!

EEEEP

THE KING'S TRICKY PLAN HAD WORKED. PERSEUS HAD AGREED TO A TASK THAT MANY HAD TRIED BEFORE HIM. BUT ALL HAD FAILED...

EMBARRASSED HE HAD BEEN SO FOOLISH, PERSEUS SECRETLY SLIPPED AWAY IN HIS BOAT TO MEDUSA'S ISLAND AND WHAT HE WAS SURE WOULD BE HIS DEATH.

ROW, ROW, ROW MY BOAT, GENTLY TO MY DOOM...

LUCKILY FOR PERSEUS, HIS POP (ZEUS) WASN'T ABOUT TO LET HIM GO AGAINST MEDUSA WITHOUT A LITTLE HELP.

HUH?

FLASH

ATHENA AND HERMES!

HEY THERE ½ BRO.

WE'RE HERE TO HELP!

BEFORE PERSEUS COULD SAY ANOTHER WORD HE WAS WHISKED AWAY TO A STRANGE GRAY LAND (NOT MEDUSA'S ISLAND).

EEEEK

SO... UM... IS THIS WHERE I'M GOING TO WAIT WHILE YOU GO SLAY MEDUSA?

NO, SILLY, YOU'RE THE ONE WHO AGREED TO SLAY MEDUSA. SO YOU NEED TO DO IT YOURSELF.

AND TO DO IT YOU'LL NEED SOME MAGICAL GIFTS FROM THE NYMPHS OF THE NORTH!

BUT THE ONLY ONES WHO KNOW HOW TO FIND THEM ARE OVER THERE. THAT'S WHY WE'VE COME HERE.

SO, GO GET DIRECTIONS!

PERSEUS DID AS HE WAS TOLD AND TIP-TOED OVER TO THE THREE GRAY LADIES. (WHO ONLY HAD ONE EYE THAT THEY SHARED).

UM, EXCUSE ME...

OH LOOK, A LITTLE BOY!

OH BOY, WHOSE TURN IS IT TO KILL THE VISITOR?

IT'S MINE!

OKAY, HERE'S THE EYE!

EEEP

FEARING FOR HIS LIFE, PERSEUS DID THE FIRST THING THAT CAME TO MIND.

ARRR

EEEEEK WHAT HAPPENED?

MY PATENTED PIRATE FISH EYE GRAB HAPPENED. AND IF YOU EVER WANT TO SEE AGAIN YOU'LL TELL ME WHAT I WANT TO KNOW!

OKAY OKAY

ONCE PERSEUS GOT THE DIRECTIONS, THEY WERE ON THEIR WAY TO THE EXOTIC LAND THE NYMPHS OF THE NORTH CALLED HOME!

HOORAY, WE HAVE VISITORS!

WE NEVER GET VISITORS!

BECAUSE THE NYMPHS WERE SO EXCITED TO HAVE GUESTS THEY PRESENTED THEM WITH THREE MAGICAL GIFTS (JUST LIKE ATHENA AND HERMES KNEW THEY WOULD). THEY WERE: AN EMPTY MAGICAL BAG, A BRAND-NEW INVISIBLE CAP, AND FLYING SANDALS.

THANKS EVERYONE!

OKAY, HAPPY BOY. TIME TO GO!

OFF TO YOUR DOOM!

MEDUSA'S HOUSE
OF ROCK

INSIDE HER CAVE

WHEN PERSEUS FINALLY RETURNED HOME (WITH HIS NEW GIRLFRIEND) HE HEADED STRAIGHT TO KING POLYDECTES' PALACE.

UPON ENTERING HE WAS SHOCKED TO FIND HE WAS INTERRUPTING A WEDDING!

MOM!

HELP, PERSEUS!

PERSEUS!

GRRRR LADIES, COVER YOUR EYES. IT'S ABOUT TO GET UGLY!

HERE'S YOUR FAVOR, KING!

ARGG!

FLASH

111

114

115

116

A FEW MOMENTS LATER (INSIDE).

HEE HEE HEE OH YES I DID!

SAY DAD, I NEED TO TELL YOU SOMETHING!

SURE SON, BUT CAN IT WAIT ONE MORE SECOND?

OKAY?

GOOD, 'CAUSE I GOT YOU A PRESENT.

COOL WHAT IS IT?

IT'S A NEIGHBOR STABBER!

GEE, IT'S AWESOME, DAD.

NOW, WHAT DID YOU WANT TO TELL ME?

UM... I'M IN LOVE WITH THE NEIGHBOR GIRL AND WE WANT TO GET MARRIED.

HA HA HA HA HA THAT'S A GOOD ONE, SON NOW LET'S GO PRACTICE STABBING!

ONCE PYRAMUS REALIZED THAT STANDING UP TO HIS FATHER WASN'T GOING TO WORK, HE GOT DEPRESSED... AND HAD HIMSELF A GOOD LONG CRY.

SOB SOB SOB

HE THEN TRIED TO CHEER HIMSELF UP BY THINKING OF CREATIVE WAYS HE AND THISBE COULD SECRETLY EXPRESS THEIR FEELINGS WHENEVER THEY SAW EACH OTHER IN THE MARKETPLACE.

HMMM...

IDEAS JOURNAL

FEELINGS JOURNAL
POEMS BY PYRAMUS
SONGS FOR THISBE
PRETTY DRAWINGS

HIS FIRST IDEA FAILED MISERABLY BECAUSE IT WAS A BIT TOO OBVIOUS.

WOW MOM, THIS MULBERRY JAM IS SOOO BEAUTIFUL!

HEY MOM, THIS MULBERRY JAM IS SO HANDSOME! IF ONLY I COULD MARRY IT!

JAM STA

WHITE MULBERRY JAM

I DISAGREE, PYRAMUS, I THINK IT'S UGLY!

THISBE, YOU'RE TOO GOOD FOR THAT JAM!

HIS SECOND IDEA INVOLVED A SECRET CODE AND WORKED MUCH BETTER!

IT WAS A STRANGE YET SIMPLE CODE. FOR INSTANCE, A SIMPLE "COUGH" MEANT "I LOVE YOU!"

PYRAMUS!

COUGH COUGH

PIES

THISBE!

COUGH COUGH COUGH

AND IF THEY WANTED TO SAY "OUR LOVE WILL BRING US TOGETHER FOREVER," ALL THEY NEEDED TO DO WAS LIE ON THE GROUND AND FLAIL THEIR ARMS AND LEGS.

OH MY!

HELP

COUGH COUGH

COUGH COUGH

THE CODE DID HAVE ITS FLAWS, BUT IT WAS ALL THEY HAD.

120

FRIGHTENED, THISBE RAN OFF INTO THE WOODS, TO WAIT FOR THE LIONESS TO FINISH HER DINNER...

EEEEEEK

SQUAWK

SQUAWK

EEEP

WHICH SHE DID.

AHHH

THEN SHE CLEANED UP AND LEFT.

124

NEARBY, THISBE DECIDED IT WAS TIME TO GO BACK TO SEE IF THE LIONESS WAS GONE OR IF HER LOVE HAD ARRIVED YET.

HE HAD!

EEEEK

RIGHT AWAY SHE KNEW WHAT HAD HAPPENED!

THE LIONESS ATE THE CHICKEN AND THEN STABBED YOU!

THISBE... I...I... COUGH COUGH

I LOVE YOU TOO, PYRAMUS. WAIT FOR ME, MY LOVE

KER PLUNK

125

SO IT WAS, THE TWO YOUNG LOVERS DIED TOGETHER UNDER THE BLOODSTAINED WHITE MULBERRY TREE.

AND FROM THAT DAY FORTH ALL MULBERRY TREES MYSTERIOUSLY YIELDED RED BERRIES INSTEAD OF WHITE!

SOB SOB
I'LL TAKE ONE BEAUTIFUL JAR, PLEASE.

SOB SOB
AND I'LL TAKE ONE HANDSOME JAR.

NEW RED

IN THE END, THEIR PARENTS DECIDED TO HONOR THEIR CHILDREN'S LOVE AND MIXED THEIR ASHES TOGETHER IN ONE URN. NOW THEY TRULY WOULD BE TOGETHER FOREVER.

SOB SOB SOB

HOORAY FOR LOVE!

THE URN

YEAH!

SOB SOB SOB

THE SAD-TASTIC END

ONCE UPON AN ISLAND, CALLED CRETE, THERE LIVED A KING NAMED MINOS...

WHO LIVED IN A BEAUTIFUL PALACE...

THAT WAS DESIGNED BY A WORLD RENOWNED ARCHITECT AND INVENTOR NAMED DAEDALUS.

THAT'S ME.

THE KING ALSO HAD DAEDALUS DESIGN AND BUILD AN INESCAPABLE MAZE UNDER THE PALACE CALLED THE...

LABYRINTH.

ITS PURPOSE WAS TO HOUSE THE KING'S HALF-MAN, HALF-BULL STEP-SON, THE MINOTAUR.

THAT'S ME!

MINOS WAS VERY PLEASED WITH DAEDALUS'S WORK... UNTIL A YOUNG HERO NAMED THESEUS KILLED THE MINOTAUR...

ESCAPED THE MAZE...

AND RAN OFF WITH THE KING'S DAUGHTER.

THIS MADE KING MINOS ABSOLUTELY FURIOUS AND HE KNEW THAT THE ONLY WAY THE YOUNG HERO COULD HAVE ESCAPED WAS WITH THE HELP OF...

DAEDALUS!

SO, TO PUNISH THE INVENTOR-ARCHITECT, THE KING DECIDED TO MAKE HIM AND HIS SON, ICARUS, HIS PRISONERS.

THEY WERE ALLOWED TO MOVE ABOUT CRETE FREELY, THEY JUST COULDN'T LEAVE THE ISLAND.

SINCE DAEDALUS DIDN'T WANT HIS SON TO SPEND HIS LIFE AS A PRISONER, HE BEGAN WORK IMMEDIATELY ON AN ESCAPE PLAN HE CALLED...

CRANK CRANK CRANK

TWEET TWEET

S N A P

TWEET!

OPERATION FREEDOM FLIES!

129

IT WAS A GOOD PLAN, ALTHOUGH A BIT STRANGE.

HEY DAD I'M HOME!

WHATCHA DOING?

OH, HI SON. I'M JUST FINISHING UP PHASE ONE OF "OPERATION FREEDOM FLIES."

HEY, IF YOU HAVE A SECOND I COULD SURE USE SOME HELP!

SORRY DAD, I CAN'T. I'M GOING TO GO WORK ON **MY OWN** ESCAPE PLAN, AND IT DOESN'T INVOLVE A BUNCH OF SILLY BIRDS.

TWEET

UM... WHAT'S YOUR PLAN, ICARUS?

WELL, IF YOU MUST KNOW, I'VE BEEN SECRETLY TRAINING A BUNCH OF MONKEYS...

TO FIGHT LIKE AN ARMY OF WARRIORS!

COME ON IN, GUYS!

131

132

ONCE IN HIS ROOM, ICARUS HANDED OUT COPIES OF THE THEME SONG'S MUSIC AND LYRICS, THEN BEGAN THE REHEARSAL.

OKAY GUYS, I'LL SING IT THROUGH ONCE, THEN YOU CAN JOIN IN WHEN YOU FEEL READY!

AHEM...

IF YOU NEED-A HAND-A WE WORK FOR BANANAS WE'RE THE MONKEY ARMY! NO NEED TO ALARMY 'CAUSE WE'RE THE MONKEY ARMY!

BUT BEFORE ICARUS EVEN GOT TO THE SECOND VERSE... THERE WAS A STRANGE INTERRUPTION.

SQUAWK SQUAWK SQUA SQUAWK

HUH?

SQUAWK

HEY DAD!

WHAT IN THE WORLD ARE YOU DOING OUT HERE?

OH, I'M JUST WORKING ON PHASE TWO OF OPERATION FREEDOM FLIES!

SQUAWK!

PLUCK

FEATHERS

WELL, CAN YOU KEEP IT DOWN? BECAUSE I STILL HAVE A LOT OF WORK TO DO BEFORE NOON TOMORROW!

WHAT'S HAPPENING AT NOON TOMORROW, ICARUS?

WE'RE ATTACKING THE GUARDS OF COURSE!

OH WOW, THAT SOON! WELL, I GUESS I BETTER TELL YOU THAT I JUST CAN'T LET YOU DO IT... I'M AFRAID YOU'LL GET HURT!

GASP!

YOU STINK DAD!

I'M GOING TO MY ROOM!

OH, AND I HATE YOU!

SLAM

SIGH

I BETTER FINISH MY PLAN TONIGHT... BEFORE ICARUS DOES SOMETHING STUPID!

AS NIGHT FELL DAEDALUS WAS STILL HARD AT WORK ON PHASE THREE (MAKING LARGE, LIGHT-WEIGHT FRAMES).

FEATHERS

HE THEN MOVED RIGHT INTO THE FOURTH AND FINAL PHASE (COVERING THE FRAMES WITH FEATHERS, USING HOT WAX AS GLUE).

AND BY THE TIME THE MORNING SUN BEGAN TO RISE... OPERATION FREEDOM FLIES WAS DONE.

HEY ICARUS, WAKE UP.

HUH? WHAT DO YOU WANT NOW, DAD?

DID YOU WANT TO TELL ME I CAN NO LONGER BREATHE?

NO, I WANTED TO SHOW YOU SOMETHING.

WHOA!

WHAT ARE THOSE?

THEY'RE WINGS!

Z Z Z Z Z

136

138

OFF IN THE DISTANCE DAEDALUS COULD ONLY WATCH IN HORROR AS HIS SON FELL TO HIS DEATH.

NOOOOOO!

BECAUSE THERE WAS NOTHING HE COULD DO!

SOB SOB SOB

DAEDALUS WAS SAD.

BUT ON A MORE HAPPY NOTE... WHEN THE MONKEY ARMY FINALLY AWOKE AND FOUND ICARUS GONE. THEY DECIDED NOT TO ATTEMPT THE DANGEROUS ESCAPE FROM CRETE.

YAWN

Z   Z

AND THEY LIVED HAPPILY EVER AFTER!

THE KER PLUNKING END

STORY #NINE

HERCULES
1. 2. 3.   4. 5. 6. 7. 8.
AND THE TEN LABORS
9. 10. (GIVE OR TAKE A FEW) 11. 12.

STARRING

HERCULES AND HIS HUGE MUSCLES

ZEUS AND HERA

PLUS HERCULES' COUSIN-KING EURYSTHEUS AND HIS TINY MUSCLES

PLEASE ENJOY →

142

IT SEEMED LIKE NOTHING COULD STOP HERCULES, NOT EVEN THE MOST VICIOUS BEAST IN ALL OF HIS HOMETOWN OF THEBES.

AGE 25

GROWL

OH BOY, FINALLY A JACKET!

THESPIAN LION

CR SMACK GROWL CRACK HEE HEE

HEY EVERYONE, CHECK OUT MY NEW JACKET!

LOOK EVERYONE!

HERCULES KILLED THE THESPIAN LION!

THE PEOPLE OF THEBES WERE SO PLEASED WITH HERCULES.

HOORAY   YAY   HOORAY

THAT THEY REWARDED HIM WITH THEIR BEAUTIFUL PRINCESS, MEGARA, FOR A WIFE!

HERCULES IS HAPPY!

OVER THE NEXT FEW YEARS HERCULES' FAMILY GREW AND HE WAS VERY HAPPY.

BOYS! TIME TO WASH UP FOR DINNER!

WHEN HERA FOUND OUT ABOUT HOW GREAT THINGS WERE WITH HERCULES...

HEY HERA, LOOK HOW HAPPY MY HEROIC SON AND HIS FAMILY ARE!

HERA'S REALLY FAKE SMILE

SHE DECIDED THAT BEFORE SHE COULD TRY KILLING HIM AGAIN SHE SHOULD FIRST TRY TO DESTROY HIS FAMILY AND HEROIC STATUS. HER PLAN...

...TO INFLICT HERCULES WITH AN EVIL MADNESS

HEE HEE

145

THIS MADNESS MADE HIM DO SOME...

DADDY?

...HORRIBLE...

CENSORED

CENSORED

...HORRIBLE THINGS.

CENSORED

CENSORED

WHEN THE MADNESS FINALLY LEFT HERCULES, HE FOUND HIMSELF STANDING IN HIS HOME IN UTTER SHOCK AT WHAT HE SAW.

I....I....MUST'VE KILLED MY ENTIRE FAMILY!

UPSET BEYOND BELIEF, THE NOW FAMILY-LESS HERCULES RAN UN-HEROICALLY OUT OF TOWN TO GO FIND AN ORACLE TO ASK FOR HELP AND ADVICE.

HERCULES IS HEARTBROKEN

SOB SOB

HERA'S REAL SMILE

THE ORACLE OF DELPHI'S PLACE

SOB SOB SOB

ONCE HERCULES ARRIVED HE EXPLAINED EVERYTHING THAT HAD HAPPENED TO THE ORACLE...

HMMM... LET'S SEE

EVEN THOUGH YOU DIDN'T KNOW WHAT YOU WERE DOING, YOU MUST STILL GO TO YOUR COUSIN'S AND COMPLETE WHATEVER TEN LABORS HE GIVES YOU TO DO!

THEN YOU WILL BE PURIFIED FOR YOUR HORRIBLE DEEDS.

HERCULES WILL DO IT!

147

HERCULES' COUSIN EURYSTHEUS WAS A TINY LITTLE MUSCLE-LESS KING WHO RULED THE LAND OF MYCENAE.

HERCULES! WHAT ARE YOU DOING HERE?

I'VE COME TO ASK YOU TO GIVE ME TEN DIFFICULT LABORS TO DO!

REALLY?

YUP

SINCE THE KING HATED HIS MUSCLE-COVERED COUSIN SO MUCH, HE HAPPILY SAID YES AND WITH THE HELP OF HIS ADVISORS HE SET TO WORK MAKING A LIST.

I KNOW, LET'S MAKE HIM MARRY A PIG!

HA HA HA NO. I DON'T WANT TO JUST EMBARRASS HIM, I WANT HIM **TO DIE!**

IDEAS

SO, AFTER HOURS OF SUGGESTIONS AND EVIL LAUGHTER...

HEE

HARDY-HAR

GIGGLE

HEE HEE

TE-HE

HO-HO

HA HA

HA HA

THE KING HAD FINISHED HIS LIST.

WELL, HERE YOU GO! ENJOY! HEE HEE

HERCULES WILL DO IT!!!

HERCULES EAGERLY WENT STRAIGHT TO WORK ON THE LIST, NOT ONCE STOPPING TO THINK ABOUT HOW IMPOSSIBLE AND DEADLY THE LABORS WERE.

LABOR #1- KILL THE NEMEAN LION...

GROWL

GRRR

!

WHO WAS A LION THAT NO WEAPON COULD PIERCE...

GRR

GROWL

STAB #

HUH?

GROWL

SO HERCULES... JUST HUGGED HIM TO DEATH.

SO SOFT!

LABOR #2- SLAY THE NINE-HEADED HYDRA (WITH DEADLY STINKY BREATH).

STINKY

POW

LABOR #3- CAPTURE ARTEMIS'S SACRED STAG... **ALIVE!**

SO AS NOT TO HARM HIM (WITH HIS BRUTE STRENGTH), HERCULES SIMPLY CHASED HIM FOR AN ENTIRE YEAR...

UNTIL THE SACRED STAG WAS WORN OUT.

HERCULES LIKES YOUR BREATH MUCH MORE THAN THE HYDRA'S!

LABOR #4- KILL THE HUGE BOAR THAT LIVED ON MOUNT ERYMANTHUS.

GRRR

GROWL

SMASH

HERCULES FOUND THIS TASK A LITTLE TOO EASY AND A BIT...

BOARING

LABOR #5- CLEAN KING AUGEAS'S STABLES OUT IN ONE DAY... A SEEMINGLY IMPOSSIBLE TASK, EVEN FOR AN ARMY OF MEN...

BUT HERCULES JUST USED HIS MUSCLES AND SOME BOULDERS TO DIVERT TWO RIVERS INTO THE STABLES, MAKING CLEANING...

MOO!

MOO!

MOO!

MOO!

NO PROBLEM!

150

LABOR #6- SAVE THE TOWN OF STYMPHALUS FROM THE THOUSANDS UPON THOUSANDS OF DANGEROUS STYMPHALIAN BIRDS.

SQUAWK

HERCULES IS GOING TO NEED MORE ARROWS!

ALL DONE!

LABOR #7- CAPTURE A HUGE WILD AND CRAZY BULL FROM CRETE!

HERC-A-DOODLE-DOO I GOT YOU!

LABOR #8- DEFEAT THE EVIL KING DIOMEDES OF THRACE AND RETRIEVE HIS MAN-EATING HORSES.

ARRR

CRASH BOOM WHAM POW

HERCULES HOPES YOU GUYS ARE HUNGRY!

151

152

BY THE TIME HERCULES HAD FINISHED HIS TEN LABORS HIS DEEDS WERE, AGAIN, BEING CELEBRATED IN HIS HOMETOWN OF THEBES AND ALL OVER THE WORLD...

HEY, DID YOU GUYS HEAR ABOUT HERCULES' NEWEST HEROIC DEEDS?

YUP YUP YUP

EVEN THE GODS ON MOUNT OLYMPUS WERE ABUZZ.

HEY ZEUS, DID YOU HEAR ABOUT HERCULES' NEWEST HEROIC DEEDS?

YUP!

HUH?

HERA WAS ENRAGED...

GRRRR

AND SET OUT TO TRY TO FIX THINGS, SHE BEGAN BY GIVING KING EURYSTHEUS SOME ADVICE.

WHISPER WHISPER

HEY COUSIN, I'M BACK AND I'M DONE WITH MY LABORS.

NO YOU'RE NOT! FOR REASONS ONLY A REALLY SMART PERSON LIKE MYSELF COULD UNDERSTAND YOU NEED TO DO TWO MORE.

WHATEVER

LABORS #11 AND #12 WERE THE HARDEST YET! THE FIRST WAS TO RETRIEVE THE HESPERIDES' APPLES. THEY WERE SPECIAL APPLES THAT COULD ONLY BE PICKED BY A GOD.

THE APPLES

HMMM...

A DEAD 100-HEADED DRAGON.

SO WHEN HERCULES NOTICED THAT THE GOD ATLAS WAS NEARBY (HE HAD THE DUTY OF HOLDING UP THE HEAVENS) HE APPROACHED HIM FOR A FAVOR.

SURE I'D DO IT, IF I WASN'T A BIT BUSY.

WHAT IF HERCULES HELD UP THE HEAVENS?

REALLY? OKAY!

WHEN ATLAS CAME BACK WITH THE APPLES HE DECIDED HE DIDN'T WANT TO RETURN TO HIS OLD JOB AND TOLD HERCULES. SO HERCULES HAD TO THINK QUICK.

NO PROBLEM ATLAS, BUT BEFORE YOU LEAVE, CAN YOU SCRATCH MY BUM? HERCULES HAS AN ITCH.

UMM... HOW ABOUT I HOLD THE HEAVENS UP FOR A SEC. AND YOU SCRATCH YOUR BUM YOURSELF.

OKAY!

I'M AN IDIOT!

HEE HEE

LABOR #11 WAS COMPLETE!

154

THE LAST LABOR—#12— WAS TO RETRIEVE HADES' THREE-HEADED DOGGY, CERBERUS.

HA HA HA SURE HERC, YOU CAN TRY AND CATCH MY DOGGY... JUST NO WEAPONS!

AND CATCH HIM HE DID...

OWWLLL

HOWLLL!

HOWLLL!

BUT NOT BEFORE HIS LONGEST, TOUGHEST STRUGGLE YET.

A SHORT TIME LATER BACK AT KING EURYSTHEUS'S PALACE.

OKAY, OKAY, YOU COMPLETED YOUR TASKS. YOU'RE FREE, JUST TAKE THAT DOGGY AND GO!

NOPE, THAT WASN'T PART OF THE DEAL. BYE, BYE.

AND SO IT WAS, HERCULES WAS PURIFIED FROM HIS EVIL DEEDS!

EEEEKKK BAD DOGGY

HEE HEE

155

NOW LAST, BUT NOT LEAST, HERCULES...

LISTEN KIDS, SHOES DON'T MAKE THE MAN... **BUT**...

EVIL FIGHTING FERRETS

HISSS

KER SMACK

A MAN **CAN** MAKE HIS SHOES!

AND HERCULES' FINAL CLOSING THOUGHT INVOLVES A CERTAIN STUPID SHEEP'S MOTHER...

THIS SHEEP'S MOTHER LOOKS JUST LIKE THAT SHRUBBERY!

REALLY? WHICH ONE?

THE REALLY, REALLY BIG ONE!

THE END

HA HA HA HA HA

GRRR

160